MOSES

and the

ANGELS

MOSES

and the

ANGELS

by Ileene Smith Sobel
Paintings by Mark Podwal

With an Introduction by Elie Wiesel

DELACORTE PRESS

Published by Delacorte Press
Bantam Doubleday Dell Publishing Group, Inc.
1540 Broadway
New York, New York 10036

Library of Congress Cataloging in Publication Data
    Sobel, Ileene Smith.
        Moses and the angels / by Ileene Smith Sobel; illustrated by Mark Podwal.
            p.   cm.
        Includes bibliographical references.
        Summary: Describes the events in the life of Moses and the
    presence of angels as a sign of God's special relationship to this prophet.
        ISBN 0-385-32612-2
        1. Moses (Biblical leader)—Juvenile literature.   2. Moses (Biblical leader) in
    rabbinical literature—Juvenile literature.   3. Bible. O.T.—Biography—Juvenile
    literature.   4. Angels (Judaism)—Juvenile literature.   [1. Moses (Biblical leader)
    2. Angels.]   I. Podwal, Mark H., ill.   II. Title.
    BM580.M6S63 1998
    296.1′9—dc21   98-5125
                                                                    CIP
                                                                    AC

Book design by Susan Clark Dominguez
MANUFACTURED IN THE UNITED STATES OF AMERICA
March 1999
BVG   10 9 8 7 6 5 4 3 2 1

For Nathaniel and Rebecca,
angels both —I.S.S.

For David —M.P.

"HIS MEMORY SHALL BE CELEBRATED AS LONG AS THE WORLD LASTS, AND NOT ONLY AMONG THE HEBREWS, BUT AMONG ALL PEOPLES."

—*God speaking to Amram, Moses' father, in a dream*

CONTENTS

INTRODUCTION

Moses and Pharaoh, Moses and his people, Moses and the angels. A thousand and one tales, miraculous and inspiring, exist in the universe of commentaries about this singular biblical leader whose destiny marks a turning point for Israel and the world. The reader will find many of them evoked in this enchanting volume. Beautifully told by Ileene Smith Sobel and marvelously illustrated by Mark Podwal, *Moses and the Angels* appeals to the moral imagination of the child, as well as to the adult who dreams of ancient times and magical beginnings.

Magical, thus mystical, evolving on the other side of reality, is the glorious legend of "our teacher Moses," from his birth to his final day as prophet and lawgiver.

At every crossroads of his life, on earth as well as in heaven, there is an inevitable celestial intervention to save him from the darkness of death or guide him toward the dazzling light of truth.

To plunge into this magnificent book is to be carried into a world of fantasy and wisdom on the burning wings of angels thirsting for eternity.

Elie Wiesel

MOSES

and the

ANGELS

1

PHARAOH AND THE ANGEL OF DREAMS

One night, Pharaoh, King of Egypt, woke trembling. The Angel of Dreams had shown him a huge balancing scale with all the pyramids of Egypt on one side and only a baby goat, a kid, on the other. Surely, the pyramids should have outweighed the goat. But in the strange world of this dream, it was the other way around.

Pharaoh gathered wise men from every part of the land to discover what his dream could mean. "It reveals that Egypt will be weakened," pronounced the sorcerer Balaam, known for his ability to see into the future. "A son of the Hebrews soon to be born is going to destroy our land." So Pharaoh decreed: *All sons born to the Children of Israel must be drowned!*

———————

One mother, Jochebed, hid her son for three months, until she could conceal him no longer. Then she placed him among the reeds beside the Nile, in a basket caulked with pitch, so that it might float. Jochebed knew her child was destined for something remarkable. At the very moment of his birth, the house, which was always so dark, had brightened with the light of the sun and moon combined.

For one week, Jochebed went to the river to nurse her infant in the night. At dawn, his sister, Miriam, would come to keep away the birds. The angels, also wanting to protect the child, appealed to God to make sure he would be found.

God responded by bringing a brutal heat upon Egypt, which sent Pharaoh's daughter down to the river. The princess was bathing in the shallows when she noticed the little basket tucked into the reeds. At first, it seemed too far to reach. Then something wondrous happened. The princess's arm became as long as a willow. Gracefully, she pulled the basket to shore.

Inside was a beautiful infant, whom the childless princess wanted to keep. But since he was probably one of the Hebrews her father had doomed, she thought she would have to abandon him. God changed the princess's

mind by dispatching the Angel Gabriel. When Gabriel struck the infant, his crying moved the princess so deeply that she decided not to give him up after all.

———————

The baby was hungry but would not take milk from any Egyptian woman. Watching from the reeds, his sister, Miriam, came forward, offering to find a Hebrew nursemaid. When Miriam returned with a woman willing to take the child, the princess said, "Here, this is yours to nurse." Pharaoh's daughter had no idea that Miriam had fetched Jochebed, the child's true mother.

———————

Jochebed raised her son until he was two. Then she brought him back to Pharaoh's daughter, as she had promised. The princess embraced the boy and called him Moses, because she had drawn him out of the water. In Hebrew, *Moses* means "to draw out."

2

THE ANGEL MICHAEL FOOLS THE EXECUTIONER

At first, Moses was treated like a true member of the royal family. Then, when he was three, he got into mischief. While dining with Pharaoh, Moses snatched the crown from the ruler's head and put it on his own.

Once again, Pharaoh gathered his wise men. "How dare he!" they cried. "He wants your throne!"

Pharaoh was about to summon the executioner when the Angel Gabriel, disguised as the sorcerer Balaam, persuaded him to wait. "Before putting the boy to death," said Gabriel, "let us place before him a glowing coal and a piece of gold. If he takes the coal, we will know he is innocent. If he prefers the gold, his ambition will be revealed."

Moses' life was once again spared when the angel invisibly steered his hand toward the coal. But from that day on, Moses stuttered. The three-year-old boy had touched the burning coal to his mouth.

In spite of his awkward speech, Moses became a brilliant student. His memory was extraordinary, refusing to hold any knowledge that was false. Moses studied history and the sciences, languages and mathematics,

with the finest tutors in the land. His favorite teacher, the Angel Zagzagel, came all the way from heaven.

————————

As a young man, Moses was increasingly troubled by the suffering of his Hebrew brothers. Often he would toil beside them, hauling bricks in the burning sun. This gained favor with Pharaoh, who thought Moses was trying to drive the slaves harder. Indeed, it was Moses who persuaded Pharaoh that the Children of Israel should not work on the Sabbath. "If a man does not grant his slave a day of rest," Moses told the ruler, "that slave will surely die."

One day Moses saw something truly unbearable: an Egyptian taskmaster harshly beating a Hebrew slave. Moses asked the angels if this taskmaster or his descendants would ever come to any good. When the angels said no, Moses killed the man. But he used no weapon, nor even the strength of his hands. Moses simply spoke God's name and the Egyptian fell dead.

Thinking no one had seen, Moses buried the taskmaster in the sand. But the next day, when Moses tried to make peace between two arguing Hebrews, they scornfully referred to the taskmaster's death. "Who are *you* to judge *us?*" they asked, their voices filled with contempt.

Upon hearing about the slain taskmaster, Pharaoh showed Moses no mercy and sentenced him to death. But when the executioner brought down his sword, the blade merely bent. Moses' neck had become a pillar of marble. To confuse the executioner even more, the Angel Michael appeared, looking exactly like Moses. While the executioner pursued the angel, another angel brought Moses to Ethiopia, where he would be safe.

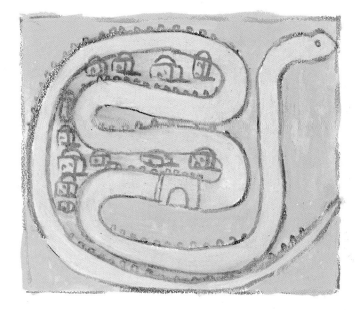

Impressed with Moses' stature and the wisdom in his face, the Ethiopians made him their ruler when their own king died. Early in his reign, Moses proved himself by cleverly arming his soldiers with storks. The menacing serpents guarding the enemy city of the sorcerer Balaam had no chance against the hungry birds.

Moses remained king for many years, until he saw that the Ethiopians wanted him to pray to their gods. He left the country because he was willing to pray only to the God of Abraham, Isaac and Jacob.

3

ANGELS OF THE
SEVEN HEAVENS

By the time Moses reached the land of Mid-ian, he yearned for a more peaceful life. At a well, he saw a beautiful young woman, and knew at once that he wanted to marry her. She was one of the shepherd Jethro's seven daughters. Zipporah was her name.

To gain her father's consent, Moses had to pull a mysterious sapphire rod from the soil of Jethro's garden. Jethro did not expect Moses to succeed, since the rod, which came from the Garden of Eden, had devoured everyone who had tried to uproot it.

But Moses prevailed. This startled Jethro to such an extent that instead of giving his consent to the marriage, he threw Moses into a pit.

For seven years, Zipporah kept Moses alive by secretly bringing him food. Then, one day, she said to her father, "Remember the man you threw into the pit? If God has allowed him to survive, would that not prove that he is blessed, and that our marriage would also be blessed?"

Jethro looked down into the pit and saw that Moses had indeed survived. After pulling Moses out of its depths, Jethro, at last, consented to the marriage. One hundred twenty thousand angels danced at the wedding. Moses and Zipporah later had two sons, Gershom and Eliezer.

Moses tended his father-in-law's sheep with the sapphire rod as his staff and an angel, appearing as a great white wolf, by his side. Moses was such a good shepherd that in forty years, not a single one of Jethro's sheep was ever attacked by a wild beast. But there was a time when one of Jethro's sheep did run off.

Afraid the creature would be lost, Moses followed it to a distant stream, where it was lapping water. "I am so sorry you were thirsty," said he, gently lifting the sheep and carrying it all the way back to the flock. God told the angels, "This shepherd is so faithful, I will entrust my flock, the Hebrew people, to him."

———————

Moses was tending his sheep at the foot of Mount Horeb when he came upon an amazing sight, a thorn-bush that would not burn up even though it was in

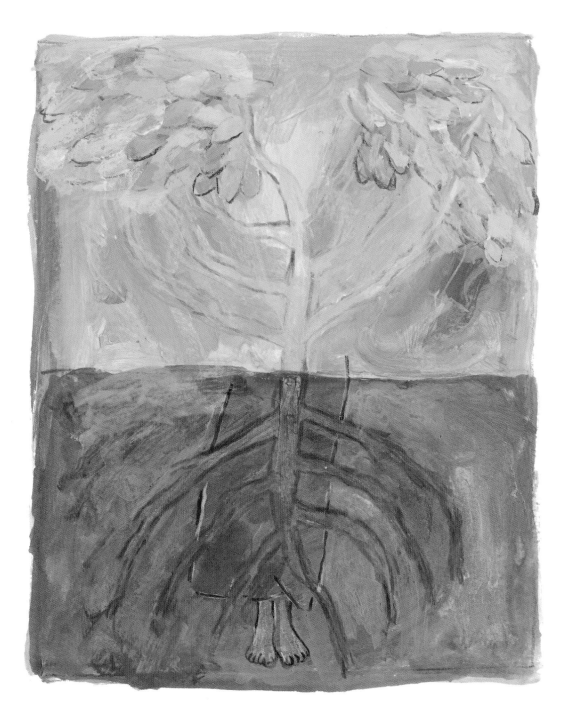

flames. When Moses looked around, he realized that none of the other shepherds could see this wonder. It was meant for him alone.

The flames Moses saw were the fiery part of the Angel Michael, angels being made half of fire. But it was God Himself who called to Moses. God spoke in the voice of Moses' father, Amram, so that the shepherd would not be afraid. Moses saw that none of the other shepherds were aware of this voice. It was meant for him alone.

When the voice revealed itself as God the Almighty, Moses immediately covered his face. For his modesty, God rewarded Moses with an amazing journey. The Lord allowed Moses to see the Seven Heavens while he was still alive.

———————

Moses was escorted to heaven by Metatron, the Angel of the Face. But Metatron was not alone. Fifteen thousand angels flew to Moses' left, another fifteen thousand to his right.

In the first heaven, Moses saw endless pairs of windows, each guarded by its own angel. Metatron pointed out windows for tears and laughter, war and peace, poverty and riches, foolishness and cleverness. There were even windows for different kinds of weather: high winds and light breezes, downpours and mist.

In the second heaven, Moses met the Angel Nuriel and the fifty thousand angels under his command. Every one of these angels had his face turned in the identical direction. They were all looking toward God.

The third heaven was inhabited by an angel with seventy thousand heads. Each head had seventy thou-

sand tongues praising God. Metatron told Moses that this angel never slept. Not only did he look after all the fruits and grains, but he was also responsible for the leaves of every tree and each individual blade of grass.

Angels in the fourth heaven prayed for the earth, the sun, the moon and the stars, in a temple made of red, white and green fire.

The fifth heaven was filled with countless Ishim, angels made of fire and snow who existed solely to praise God.

In the sixth heaven stood a towering angel with a body made of hail. This angel was so tall that Moses could have climbed for hundreds of years without ever reaching his wings.

In the seventh and last heaven, Moses was surrounded by beautiful six-winged Seraphim when he saw an angel with a serpent's head and thousands of eyes. This had to be the Angel of Death. Moses prayed that God would not let him fall into this angel's hands, and indeed he was spared. God was not ready for Moses to be taken.

When Moses returned to the thornbush from his heavenly journey, God said to him: "Go before Pharaoh and tell him to free the Hebrew slaves. Then you will lead the Children of Israel to the Promised Land." But Moses, humble as ever, resisted. The shepherd told God that Pharaoh would never believe who had sent him.

Moses remained reluctant even after God taught him to perform wonders like turning his rod into a snake. When the shepherd, still doubtful, reminded God of his troubled speech, the Lord reassured him, "In Egypt, you will be met by your brother, Aaron, and he will speak for you."

4

THE ANGEL OF DEATH
VISITS THE EGYPTIANS

Pharaoh's palace was immense, with all four
hundred entrances guarded by pairs of
hungry lions. But as the brothers approached,
these lions became gentle as puppies, affection-
ately licking their feet. Then all the beasts
formed a great procession behind the Angel
Gabriel and escorted the two men through the
palace gates. Though Moses was eighty and
Aaron eighty-three, they stood straight as trees,

and as they entered Pharaoh's court, their faces captured the light of the sun.

It was Pharaoh's birthday, and rulers were arriving from far-off lands to crown him King of the World. When Moses and Aaron stood before his throne with no crown in hand, Pharaoh demanded to know why they had come.

"The Lord sent us to tell you, *Free the Hebrew slaves!*" said the brothers.

"The Lord?" repeated Pharaoh. "Impossible. *I* am Lord of the Universe!"

"We mean the Lord who created the world in seven days," said the brothers.

"Do not mock me," said Pharaoh, still disbelieving.

So Aaron threw down his rod, turning it into a snake. "Any Egyptian schoolchild can perform that trick," said Pharaoh.

Suddenly, there were children everywhere turning rods into snakes, just as Pharaoh had said.

So Aaron performed another wonder, making his snake devour all the other snakes. Still, Pharaoh was unimpressed. He said it was natural for snakes to devour other snakes. It was only when Aaron's rod swallowed all the other rods, without becoming thicker, that Pharaoh began to worry. What if the magical rod devoured his entire palace, including his throne?

Not wanting to seem fearful, Pharaoh increased the suffering of the Hebrew slaves. He even reversed his decision about the Sabbath, forcing the Hebrews to work on the seventh day as well.

"Why did You send me back to Egypt?" Moses asked God. "Since I came to Pharaoh to speak in Your name, he has only treated the Hebrews worse."

"You will soon see what I will do to Pharaoh!" answered the Lord.

————————————

God told Moses to threaten Pharaoh, to say he would turn the waters of the Nile into blood unless the Hebrew slaves were freed. When Pharaoh refused, Aaron raised his rod and struck the waters. Moses would not do this himself, since it was the river that had saved him as an infant.

Suddenly, all the water in Egypt turned thick and red, not only in the river but also in every pitcher and cup. God met each refusal to free the Children of Israel with another plague. Only the Hebrews and one Egyptian woman, Pharaoh's daughter, were spared.

————————————

After the plague of blood, frogs swarmed over the land.

Dust turned to lice.

Lions, wolves and bears attacked every home.

Pestilence killed all the cattle, horses, camels and sheep.

Boils broke out on everyone's skin.

Fiery hail struck down all the trees.

Locusts with the jaws of lions ate every leaf and blade of grass till nothing green was left in the land.

A darkness that rose from hell made it impossible to see or even to move.

Then, near midnight, God brought the tenth plague. The Angel of Death struck down all the firstborn of Egypt.

————————————

This angel, whom Moses had encountered in heaven, was so terrifying, with his thousands of glaring eyes and serpent's head, that his victims' mouths would fall open, allowing poison from the tip of his sword to drop in.

When Pharaoh heard the wailing of his people rising over the land and discovered that his own son had died,

he knew he could endure no more. Pharaoh summoned Moses and Aaron. *"Go at once!"* he said. *"Remove the Children of Israel from this land!"* Pharaoh was so desperate that he told the Hebrews to take whatever they wanted, even silver and gold.

Moses gathered the Children of Israel and said, "Remember this day when God freed you from the land of Egypt."

5

UZZA,
ANGEL OF EGYPT,
AT THE RED SEA

The Hebrews set out on their journey with angels leading the way. By day, an angel appeared as a pillar of cloud to shelter the people and protect them from the sun. By night, another angel became a pillar of fire, to light the way.

Pharaoh soon regretted having freed the slaves. "What have I done?" he cried. But it was too late. The Hebrews were gone.

Wanting to please Pharaoh, the evil Angel Samael provided the Egyptians with six hundred of his swiftest chariots. Thus in a single day, Pharaoh's soldiers managed to overtake the Hebrews, who had left three days before.

The Hebrews were camped beside the Red Sea when they saw Pharaoh's army on the horizon. What frightened them most was the sight of Uzza, Guardian Angel of Egypt, flying wildly through the air. In terror they cried out to Moses, "Why have you brought us here to die in the wilderness?"

"Do not fear," said Moses. "The Lord will save you. Never will you see the Egyptians again."

———————————

To hold back Pharaoh's soldiers, the Angel Michael became a blazing wall of fire. The Egyptians tried to penetrate the flames with their arrows. But angels caught every one in midair.

The Egyptians still behind the flames, God told Moses to raise his staff over the Red Sea. Then, with a mighty wind, God blew back the waters, enabling the Children of Israel to walk through the middle of the sea on dry ground. The parted waters swelled to a height of sixteen hundred miles, and could be seen by every nation of the earth.

The Angel Gabriel, who had arrived with Michael, was about to take revenge on the Egyptians when Uzza, Angel of Egypt, begged for mercy. While God considered his plea, the Angel Gabriel flew to Egypt, returning with one of the newborns drowned long ago by Pharaoh's decree. Looking upon the tragic sight, God decided to punish the Egyptians.

Now that the Children of Israel were safely across the Red Sea, God restored its waters. Then He hurled Uzza, Guardian Angel of Egypt, into its depths. Rahab, Angel of the Sea, met the same fate, for trying to defend the Egyptians.

Pharaoh's soldiers attempted to flee, but angels with swords and spears held them in place. Then God threw all the Egyptians into the sea, where they were awaited by the Angels of Destruction. Only Pharaoh survived to be dragged down to hell, in chains, by the Angel Gabriel.

To celebrate their victory over the Egyptians, the angels began to sing in praise of God. But the Lord silenced them. "My creatures have drowned," He said. "This is no time for song."

6

BREAD OF ANGELS

The Children of Israel followed Moses into the desert, only to find snakes, scorpions and lizards covering the sand. The people were frightened until God sent the Guardian Angel of the Wilderness to protect them.

After three days in the desert, the Hebrews ran out of water. At Marah, their spirits soared. Water was found. But soon it was discovered that the water was bitter. While the Hebrews grumbled about their leader, Moses spoke to God.

The Lord showed Moses a laurel tree and told him to write His name on its wood. Moses threw the wood into the water, and the people were able to drink. The water had become sweet.

When the Hebrews grew hungry and complained they had no food, God told Moses, "Do not worry. Bread will rain down from heaven for you." The next morning, the ground glistened with flakes of manna. "This is the bread of angels," Moses explained.

Manna tasted of whatever one desired. To a child manna was milk; to a young man or woman, bread; to the old, it was like honey. From manna, the Hebrews became as strong as the angels that made it in heaven. They could now continue their journey toward the Promised Land.

At Rephadim, the Children of Israel were attacked by the wicked sorcerer Amalek. Moses called upon the warrior Joshua to defend them in a battle that would be decided by sundown.

While Joshua fought, Moses stood on the top of a hill, his arms raised to God. So long as Moses kept his arms high, Joshua triumphed. But when Moses grew tired and let his arms down, Amalek prevailed.

Aaron offered his brother a cushion to sit on. But Moses would accept only a stone. Comfort was not possible while his people were suffering, though Moses did allow Aaron to hold his arms up to heaven when they became too heavy.

By sundown, Joshua had defeated the Amalekites. But only because God had given Moses extra time to hold up his arms, by making the sun stand still.

7

MOSES CONVINCES THE ANGELS

When the Children of Israel came to the wilderness of Sinai, they camped at the foot of a mountain enveloped in clouds. On the third day, trumpets blared, lightning tore open the sky, and the mountain itself shook. God sent the angels to soothe the people, who thought the world was coming to an end.

Then, in the voice of thunder, which echoed from one end of the world to the other, God told Moses to come up the mountain.

The angels Gabriel and Michael took Moses by the hand and led him into a cloud that brought him to God's throne. Moses found the Lord carving crowns into two stone tablets that contained His Laws, the Ten Commandments.

———————

God handed the tablets to Moses, but the angels wanted to keep them for themselves. Moses had to persuade the angels that mankind needed the Laws more than they did. "It is written in these Commandments," said Moses, "'I am the Lord who brought you out of Egypt.'" Moses asked the angels, "Were *you* enslaved in Egypt? It is also written, 'Remember the Sabbath day and keep it holy.' Does *your* work tire you so that *you* need a day of rest? And it says, 'Honor thy father and thy mother.' Do *you* have fathers and mothers?" Finally, the

angels gave way, allowing Moses to take the tablets down the mountain.

Moses rolled the stone tablets like a scroll and set out for Earth, with sixty thousand angels to his right and

sixty thousand to his left. These angels bore invisible crowns for the Children of Israel, who were about to receive God's Laws.

Moses' face shone with the light of heaven when he returned to his people.

8

THE EVIL ANGEL SAMAEL AND THE GOLDEN CALF

Before Moses left to receive the Command-ments, he promised the Children of Israel that he would return by noon of the forty-first day. When that day arrived, the evil Angel Samael made the Hebrews think Moses was late by pulling a curtain over the sun. Then Samael wickedly filled the sky with a picture of Moses on his deathbed, making the Hebrews doubt their leader would ever return.

Feeling abandoned, the Hebrews forced Aaron to make them an idol to guide them safely through the desert. They wanted a god they could dance around, one that would give them strength, like those worshipped by the Egyptians.

Aaron threw the people's gold into a fire, and out of the flames came a golden calf that appeared to breathe. But it was the evil Angel Samael who lived within the calf. Samael wanted to lead the Hebrews astray.

When Moses returned from heaven to find his people worshipping a false god, he became so furious that he smashed the tablets given to him by God. Then he burned the golden calf, ground it to dust and threw the dust upon the water for the people to drink. Those foolish enough to have kissed the calf, themselves turned to gold.

God wanted to give the Children of Israel another chance to follow His Laws. He commanded Moses to come up the mountain again the next morning. The Lord told Moses to bring two stone tablets to replace the ones that had been broken. The first tablets had been carved by God Himself. The second tablets were carved by Moses, according to the word of God.

When Moses came down the mountain with the new tablets, his face gave off a light so brilliant that the people had to look away. Later, Moses would cover his face with a veil whenever he returned from heaven.

9

THE ANGEL OF MERCY THWARTS BALAAM

God told Moses to make a tent for the tablets so that He could dwell among His people as they journeyed through the wilderness. Within this Tabernacle was the Ark of the Covenant, where the two sacred tablets were kept. The Ark was guarded by two golden angels that hurled lightning at enemies of the Hebrews. When the Hebrews were dying from a plague, Aaron lured the Angel of Death into the Tabernacle, which brought the suffering to an end.

As the Children of Israel advanced through the wilderness, the King of Moab grew anxious. He called upon the sorcerer Balaam to put a curse upon them so that they would not reach the Promised Land. "I know that whomever you bless is blessed," said the king, "and whomever you curse is cursed."

Balaam spent seven weeks with the wicked angels Azza and Azzazel, trying to force the Children of Israel back to Egypt. When this failed, he set out on an ass in pursuit of the Hebrews.

But soon, for no apparent reason, the animal stopped and veered off the road. When Balaam whipped the ass, it opened its mouth and spoke in the voice of a man. The ass told of a sword-wielding angel that stood in its way.

Twice more the animal started out and came to an abrupt stop. Then God allowed the sorcerer to see what the ass had seen. At the sight of the Angel of Mercy, Balaam became so flustered that he blessed the Children of Israel instead of cursing them.

To learn what awaited them in the Promised Land, Moses appointed twelve scouts, one from each tribe of the Hebrews. After forty days, the men returned, two of them carrying an enormous grapevine.

Ten of the scouts did not want to live in the Promised Land. They claimed that it was filled with giants, to whom they looked as small as grasshoppers. "How can you possibly know how you looked to them?" said God. "Perhaps *I* made you seem to them like angels."

Upon hearing the scouts' wretched report, the people sobbed and begged Moses to lead them back to Egypt. For their ingratitude, God condemned the Hebrews to wander in the desert for forty years, one year for each day the scouts had spent on their mission.

Neither Moses nor the whole generation of Hebrews whom he had led through the desert would be allowed to enter the Promised Land. Only the two truthful scouts, Joshua and Caleb, were permitted to set foot on its soil.

10

THE ANGEL METATRON
REVEALS THE FUTURE

The angels were saddened by God's decision, and debated why Moses was kept
from the Promised Land, after all he had done for
his people. They wondered if it was because of
the time Moses had disobeyed God by striking a
rock to get water. Or perhaps Moses was needed
to lead his generation in heaven. Finally, they
decided it was impossible to know God's inten-
tions, for the Almighty often behaved in mysterious ways.

By now Moses was one hundred twenty years old to the day, and God decided it was time for him to die. But first He strengthened Moses' eyes, allowing him to see into the future. Metatron, who had before shown Moses

the Seven Heavens, once again served as Moses' guide. The angel revealed to Moses the history of the Promised Land, as well as its destiny.

When Moses returned from his journey, he pleaded with God not to let him be taken by the Angel of Death. God granted Moses his last wish, and instead took his soul with a kiss. Then Moses was brought to heaven by the angels Michael and Gabriel, and Moses' beloved teacher, Zagzagel.

The Angel Semalion announced Moses' death, and the angels in heaven wept as never before. Since Creation, when they were made, this was the first time the angels did not sing.

Never again did there arise among the Children of Israel a prophet like Moses, with whom the Lord spoke as a friend, face to face.

Sources

Bialik, H. N., and Rawnitzky, Y. H., editors. *The Book of Jewish Folklore and Legends.* New York: Schocken, 1992.

Bin Gorion, Micha Joseph. *Mimekor Yisrael.* Philadelphia: Jewish Publication Society of America, 1976.

Encyclopedia Judaica. Volumes 1–16. Jerusalem: Keter, 1971–72.

Fox, Everett, translator. *The Five Books of Moses.* New York: Schocken, 1995.

Freedman, H., and Simon, Maurice, translators. *Midrash Rabbah.* Volumes 1–5. London: Soncino, 1939.

Ginzberg, Louis. *The Legends of the Jews.* Volumes 1–3. Philadelphia: Jewish Publication Society of America, 1948.

Goldstein, David. *Jewish Folklore and Legend.* London: Hamlyn, 1980.

Podwal, Mark. *The Book of Tens.* New York: Greenwillow, 1994.

Simon, Maurice, and Sperling, Harry, translators. *The Zohar.* London: Soncino, 1934.

Trachtenberg, Joshua. *Jewish Magic and Superstition*. New York: Behrman House, 1939.

Unterman, Alan. *Dictionary of Jewish Lore and Legend*. London: Thames and Hudson, 1991.

Wiesel, Elie. *Messengers of God*. New York: Random House, 1976.

ABOUT THE AUTHOR

ILEENE SMITH SOBEL has been an editor of literary books for many years. Her publishing prizes include the PEN/Roger Klein Award, the Tony Godwin Memorial Award and a Jerusalem Fellowship. She lives in New York City and northwestern Connecticut with her husband and two children.

ABOUT THE ARTIST

MARK PODWAL's drawings have appeared in *The New York Times* for the past twenty-five years, and his work is represented in the collection of the Metropolitan Museum of Art in New York. In 1996 he was named *Officier de l'Ordre des Arts et des Lettres de la République Française.*